Turbo Max

A story for siblings and friends
of children with bipolar disorder

Written by Tracy Anglada
Illustrated by Deirdre Baxendale

"At first you're happy,
And then you're mad.

It makes me worry,
It makes me sad.

And if I could,
Know what I'd do?

I'd make it bright,
Each day for you!"

Cheryl Dunham

The original version of this story was published as a black and white booklet in 2002. We are pleased to present this revised full color version. Thank you to Dierdre Baxendale for the beautiful color illustrations. Thank you to Cheryl Dunham for the poetry.

© Copyright 2008, Tracy Anglada
All rights reserved.
ISBN 978-0-9817396-0-1
Library of Congress Control Number 2008903838
Published by BPChildren, Murdock, Fl
www.bpchildren.com

Mom and Dad want me to write something. Okay . . . I'm writing. Boring!! What kind of gift is a diary anyway? The red Turbo Max remote control convertible car would be way cooler! Mom says she wants me to write down how I feel. If you ask me Mandy has enough "feelings" for all of us. Wait a minute. Maybe, I could give the diary to my sister, Mandy. Then I could still have the car. Did I mention it's a Turbo Max convertible? Don't look now but mom's smiling. A little piece of gold—I don't expect you to understand! It's Mandy's fault that Mom doesn't smile much anymore. I'm the one who tries to be good. I guess if writing in this diary makes her smile, then I'll keep doing it. Good-bye red Turbo Max remote control convertible car.

Goodbye!

It's me again. If you're here to stay I should give you a real name. Something cool though, not "Dear Diary." How about "Turbo Max"? Sweet!! I'll call you Max for short. Since we're going to be friends, I'll tell you about the gold thing. Gram says most people spend their lives searching for a pot of gold and never find it. The secret is it doesn't come all at once. She says the smart people save little bits of gold—the good things—through their whole life. Then when they're really old, like Gram, they have a whole pot full. She tells me all about her gold and says I'm one of her biggest pieces. I better start saving now just in case Gram's right.
New Friend,
Rick

You owe me big time Max! I saved your skin. Mandy woke up in one of her moods. What a GRUMP! When Mom told her to brush her teeth, she blew a fuse and totally trashed the bathroom. There's toilet paper and tooth-paste everywhere. Then she came in my room and tried to shred you. I grabbed you back just in time. Don't feel too bad. She would have ripped up anything. Better hide you from now on. I have to stay in my room till Mandy calms down—that's the rule. Guess I'll be here awhile! Hope the whole summer isn't this way. Even Mrs. Grants 4th grade class last year would be better than stuck in my room. At least I have you to talk to. Hope I don't have to clean up the bathroom!

Your Rescuer,
Rick

Check this out Max. How cool! I want to enter that race but I need 12 bucks for the entry fee. Think I can come up with the money in time? Maybe Mandy will lend me some. It's a long shot but I just have to win that car. This could be a whole gold mine!

Racer,

Rick

How weird is this? I asked Mandy to lend me some money and she said OK! After her last blow up—you still owe me for saving you—she's been so sulky. She won't even get out of bed. When I asked her for the money she gave it all to me. 5 bucks! Sweet!! She said it didn't matter anyway and I could take her treasure box too. Can you believe it? She loves that box. We used to play pirates searching for our lost treasure. Of course she always had to be the one to find it. At least she played with me then. Now she's mean to me—twists my arm, pinches me, calls me names. I wonder if Mandy's even related to me. Maybe she's an alien from another planet who just looks like my sister. Could be! I feel strange about keeping her money but I really need it plus 7 bucks more.

Treasure Hunter,

Rick

Hate to tell you this Max but we're broke again. Bummer! Mandy came in my room in the middle of the night and took all the money back. She was rambling on and on about her 8th grade science project. She dragged me out of bed to show me her work. Like I want to see it in the middle of the night ... NOT! What's the hurry? School doesn't start till the end of August and she'll be in 6th grade not 8th. When I woke up this morning, she was still working on it. At least if she's busy maybe she'll leave me alone. Guess I'll have to ask Dad for the money.

Needing a Loan,

Rick

Can you keep a secret Max? I heard something I wasn't supposed to. I went to ask Dad about the money but his door was closed. I know I should have walked away but then I heard mom crying. I hate it when Mom cries! Dad said something about Mandy leaving for awhile. Then shock!! Dad came out of the room and ran right into me. I tried to ask about the race but he said, "Later, Later." Yeah right! When is later anyway? And what about Mandy? Where would she go? I have another secret: sometimes I wish Mandy was gone! I'm horrible for even thinking such a thing. I know you won't tell anyone. I love Mandy, but it almost seems like she's not my sister anymore. Hold on.

Someone's knocking ... YIPEE!! Dad says I get to sleep over at Gram's for a few days. I'll be glad to get away. No one will notice I'm gone anyway. You can come too. You'll like Gram.
Radar Ears,
Rick

Max, sorry I haven't written for a few days. I'm having a great time at Gram's. It would be cool to spend the rest of the summer here. No worries about anybody or anything. Lots of gold pieces! Gram takes me out for ice cream and to the movies. We could never do that if Mandy was around. She's been having too many fits lately. One time she had one in the middle of the Dairy Dream right in front of Allison —only the prettiest girl in school. I wanted to crawl under the table. We had to leave before we even ordered. How embarrassing is that! Oh, I almost forgot to tell you the best news of all. Gram entered me in the big race! Sweet!! Hope I win. Our problems are over.

Care Free,
Rick

It's terrible Max! Mandy's in the hospital. I'm rotten for having a good time here when I knew something was wrong. Wish I could make everything right. The worst part is I can't even go to the hospital yet. I hope she's okay. Please would somebody tell me what's going on? I'm not a baby! Everyone keeps whispering and when I walk in the room they stop talking. I overheard something about an ambulance and the paramedics. I'm really scared Max. Mandy must be bad sick if she's in the hospital. Uncle Greg was in the hospital and he never got to come home. I keep looking at the treasure box and wishing things were like they used to be. I don't even feel like practicing for the big race. I'm going to tell God that I'll give up the race if he'll just make Mandy better. Do you think He'll make her better Max? He's just got to!
Praying,
Rick

I'm getting ready to go see Mandy. Gram told me I shouldn't say anything that might upset her. I'm thinking maybe I shouldn't talk at all! I'm going to bring the treasure box for her to put by the bed. Maybe she'll feel better when she sees it. I'm keeping my end of the bargain. The race is in a few days but I'm not going. I'll tell you how the visit goes later.

Ready to Go,
Rick

Well Max, the hospital was really weird. It's not like any hospital I've seen. Mom and Dad looked awful. Mandy wants to come home but the doctor won't let her. She liked having her treasure box plus Gram bought her a big pink teddy bear holding some balloons. Mandy seemed a little strange, kinda spacey. Mom told me the doctors are giving her some medicine and her body has to adjust to it. Mandy slipped me a note right before we left. I didn't show Mom and Dad. I was afraid it would freak them out. Here's the note:

"Get me out of here.
They are poisaning my food.
Mom and Dad don't beleve me.
You have to save me Rick."

I'm trying to save her. She looked so helpless at the hospital. Mandy's older than me but I feel like the big brother now. I'm going home tonight. I'll try to help out around the house. Our vacation's over Max!
Big Brother,
Rick

10

It's so quiet at home without Mandy. Mom and Dad cleaned her room out. There were four whole garbage bags of junk. They bought her some new stuff for when she comes home from the hospital. Maybe if I was in the hospital I would get some new stuff too. Mom says I have to come with them when they see Mandy's doctor. Do you think I'll get sick like Mandy? Hope not!

Back Home,
Rick

I met Dr. Michaels today. I was afraid he would say something was wrong with me too. Turns out he's way cool. His desk is loaded with model cars. He says Mandy can come home soon because the new medicine is helping. I want her to come home but I just don't know if I'm ready yet. Finally I got the nerve to ask, "What's wrong with her?" Everyone stared at me like they were surprised I didn't know. Well how am I supposed to know if nobody tells me? Turns out Mandy has something called bipolar disorder. Have you ever heard of that Max? Doc says sometimes her brain goes super fast like a racer, they call that manic. Other times it goes really slow like she's stuck in the mud, that's when she's depressed. Doc says it can make her very cranky. Well I could have told them she's like that. I just didn't know you call it bipolar! I always thought she was just being a pain. Doc says that being bipolar is like trying to drive a remote control car when the controller isn't working right. No wonder she's so grouchy. He says the medicine will help fix the controls in her brain. Hope so! That reminds me, the big race is tomorrow. Try not to think about it!
Trying Hard,
Rick

Missing race day wasn't as bad as I thought. Gram called to ask if I was going. She's the best! I told her I just don't feel like it while Mandy's in the hospital. It's the truth. The car doesn't seem so important right now. Mom rented some movies for me instead. I watched them all afternoon. Gram says there's another race soon. She's going to find out when it is. Maybe we can try that one. Well, maybe.

Couch Potato,
Rick

12

We had our first official family meeting. Hope you didn't feel too left out Max. I'll fill you in on the good stuff. The best thing is I get an allowance now. Sweet!! 3 bucks every Friday plus if I take out the garbage every day I get another buck at the end of the week. Double Sweet!! I'm totally broke now. I spent all my money on a new yo-yo plus a candy bar and a key chain at the dollar store. We talked about Mandy coming home too. Mom and Dad are going to pick her up at the hospital tomorrow. I get to come too. Last thing, in case you're wondering, they said it's okay to be around Mandy. She's not contagious or anything. You can't catch bipolar from someone like a cold. Good thing. I was a little worried. Mom says Mandy was probably born with it and we just didn't know till now. Maybe I should have been born with it instead of Mandy—but I don't want it either! Just wish there wasn't any such thing as bipolar.
Reporting,
Rick

P.S. Almost forgot to tell you.
 I have to go to some meeting
Wednesday night. Sounds BORING!!

I saw her Max! She was at the meeting. Huge piece of gold!! I can hardly believe it. No … not Mandy. Allison! I'm so in love. I can't stop thinking about her. I promise I will be at every Wednesday night meeting for the rest of my life. Allison's mom runs this support group thing. Sweet!! The parents go off in one room and blah, blah. We get to have punch and cookies. I wonder if Allison has a sister with bipolar too? Next time, I'm going to get the nerve up to talk to her. Hope Mandy doesn't mess it up. Everything's been cool since she got home. She hasn't trashed anything or tried to shred you yet. I'm still hiding you just in case.

In Love,
Rick

14

Wow! I played pirates today with Mandy and she let me find the treasure box. That's gotta be a first. I told her I want to cure bipolar disorder when I grow up. She almost started crying and then she said I was the best brother in the world! Little piece of gold. Well I knew it all along—about time she figured it out. She didn't want to talk about the hospital much. Can you believe she doesn't remember half the stuff that happened? She feels a lot better but doesn't like taking her medicine. It makes her stomach sick. I told her that I like Allison. She promised not to say anything. Did I goof up, Max? Hope not! I think we can trust her now.
Sharing Secrets,
Rick

Rev up your engines, Max! We're set for the next race. Sweet!! There are two races left before school starts again. (Yuck! Don't think about school.) Mandy says she'll help me practice. Gram came over today. She says I've grown at least an inch and she found two new freckles. Hope Allison doesn't notice. I hate my freckles. We all went out for pizza and had a great time. I love pizza!!

Stuffed,
Rick

It feels like Wednesday will never come. I have to see Allison again! I'm going to invite her to the big race on Saturday so she can watch me win. I win every practice race with Mandy. Can you imagine it Max? The crowd will chant my name as I cross the finish line. "RICK! RICK! RICK!" Everyone will lift me up on their shoulders as I hold the trophy. It's going to be great! I know exactly which Turbo Max car to pick for the prize. Of course it won't be better than you, Max. Allison will be so impressed. Life is good!
Winner,
Rick

I had a weird problem with my car today, Max. Right in the middle of a practice run it lost all juice—just totally stopped. Mandy won the race. Guess the batteries needed to charge longer. Good news, tomorrow is Wednesday! Sweet!! Mandy doesn't want to go to the meeting. She says why go since she's feeling better. Well she is a lot better but her controls still get stuck sometimes. Wonder if she'll ever get totally better?

Wondering,
Rick

It's Wednesday! Gotta look my best for Allison. Do you think she'll like the red racer shirt or the blue Spiderman shirt? I'm going to do it tonight. I'm going to talk to her and invite her to the race. She'll say yes, won't she Max?
Hoping,
Rick

Bummer! Bummer! Bummer! No gold today. I wore my red racer shirt for nothing. Can you believe I wait a whole week and she's not even there! Even the peanut butter cookies didn't taste the same without her. It's not fair, Mandy didn't want to go and she had a great time. She even made some new friends. I should be happy for her. She hasn't had any friends for so long but this was supposed to be my night.

Bummed Out,
Rick

Max, Guess who showed up at the house today? ALLISON! I was still in my pajamas—of course! Can't it ever work out like I plan? She spent most of the time in Mandy's room. I spent most of the time in my closet. Not changing ... listening! I can hear everything in Mandy's room from my closet. You'll never guess what I heard. Mandy was moaning about being bipolar and having to take medicine. What a baby! Then Allison said she's bipolar too. NO WAY! I can hardly believe it. She remembers the day at the Dairy Dream. Allison said she felt bad for Mandy that day because she was just the same before she started her medicine. I never thought about feeling bad for Mandy that day. I felt too bad for me. Hope Allison didn't notice how embarrassed I was. She says things are good now but it took some time to get the medicine right. She told Mandy that even when she feels better she needs to keep taking her medicine or she'll start feeling bad again. Finally they started talking about me! Allison said she thinks my freckles are cute. Wonder if she noticed my two new ones when I told her goodbye?
Freckles,
Rick

Today's the day Max! I've waited for this all summer. I'll be coming home with a red convertible Turbo Max remote control car. I know I will. I can just feel it! Gram will pick me up early to go to Barry's Hobby Shop. The rest of the family will meet us there for the race.

Ready,
Rick

I'm steaming mad at Ryan Harris! What an idiot! Mom says the world is full of "ignorant" people. Did one of those "ignorant" people have to win MY pot of gold? Oh yeah, he won the race. My car died before the race even started. I'm glad Allison wasn't there. Dad says the batteries are shot. We were looking around in the Hobby Shop for new ones when Mandy's control got stuck in racer mode. She was singing and dancing around. She twirled right into a big display of model cars and then started laughing like a hyena. Everyone was staring at her and saying mean things. I got really mad at those people! It's not like Mandy wants to be bipolar. We left right away—without the batteries. On the way to the car Ryan, the LOSER, came over to show off his new car and trophy. Ryan said Mandy was "crazy" and should be in a "nut house." I just wanted to scream at him or slug him. Mandy's not crazy! I think he's the one who should be locked up. How can people be so mean, Max? It really hurt. I don't think Mandy heard him. Hope not anyway. Mom says I'm letting him control me by getting mad at him. Well, I just can't help it. I'm still MAD!
Steaming' Mad,
Rick

I solved the mystery, Max. I know why Mandy's getting worse and it spells big trouble. I went to put a piece of candy in the treasure box to surprise her. Turns out I'm the one who got a surprise. She's been putting her medicine in the box instead of taking it. Mandy walked in on me while I was looking in the box. She begged me not to tell and promised to start taking her medicine again. Before I could stop myself I made a pirate's swear not to tell Mom and Dad. I'm in way deep this time. I can't break a pirate's swear. I wish I hadn't made it! Maybe she'll start taking her medicine again. Doubt it! I need help big time.

Maybe Allison can talk her into telling Mom and Dad herself. I'll see Allison tomorrow at the meeting. I didn't promise not to tell her!

Detective,

Rick

━━━━━━━━━━━━━━━━━━━━━━━━━━━━━━━

No gold today Max—just a bunch of ugly rocks. Everything's a mess. The meeting was a total disaster. Mandy's still racing. I know she hasn't taken her medicine. She announced to the whole group that I'm in love with Allison. Even my freckles turned red! No way could I talk to Allison after that, let alone ask her for advice. I know the answer anyway. I have to tell Mom and Dad. I should have done it yesterday. Why is life so hard? Well here goes ...

Red Face,

Rick

Mandy's not speaking to me. She thinks I told to get even with her. Mom says I did the right thing. Why are the right choices always hard? Doc says if Mandy doesn't take her medicine she'll have to go back to the hospital. Mandy says I'll pay big time for squealing. I don't know what she's going to do but she had that look in her eye. I know it'll be bad. At least she took her medicine tonight. Gram says being brave enough to tell was a piece of gold. Funny I don't think Mandy sees it that way. I don't feel very brave either. Just crummy!

Squealer,
Rick

Not my car, Max! Anything but my car! She destroyed it, demolished it, smashed it to bits!! Now I can never win a new Turbo Max. This is the thanks I get for trying to help her? I just want to SCREAM!! How could she do this to me? I'll never forgive her!
Smashed,
Rick

I'm going to Gram's for a few days till things cool off. Of course I'll bring you too, Max. Mom wants me to come when Mandy sees the Doc. I said, "No way! I'm done with all that." Mom said, "Yes way! That's what families do." I'm not even going to think about it.

Still Mad,
Rick

I can't even enjoy Gram's house this time, Max. I'm still sick over my car. Dad looked at it to see if it could be fixed. He says it's too far gone. I have all the pieces in a box. Don't know what to do with it. Max, what if Gram is wrong? Maybe life has no gold for people like me, only people like Ryan Harris. Maybe in the end I'll just have a box full of smashed pieces.
Lost,
Rick

I got two cards in the mail today. Strange since I haven't gotten any letters all summer. Mandy sent an "I'm sorry" card. I'm sure Mom made her write it. I ripped it up! The other one is from Allison. I wanted to show it to you, Max.

This is what I'm going to write back to her—YES!!

Smiling,
Rick

We're going to see the Doc today. I'll have to see Mandy too. It's the first time since she smashed my car. I may have to see her but I'm not going to talk to her. I'll tell you how the visit goes later. Mom says it's time to come home if I'm ready. I don't know Max. Are we ready?
Not Sure,
Rick

Mandy really seems sorry about the car. I tried not to talk to her but it was harder than I thought. She's doing better now that she's taking her medicine again. Doc says I did the right thing. Mandy told him she just couldn't stand the idea of taking medicine for the rest of her life. Doc says there are lots of things he can do to help but she has to let him know what's bothering her. As for taking it the rest of her life, he says nobody knows. There are scientists and doctors and researchers all working on it. Maybe someday soon they'll find a way to cure bipolar disorder. She just needs to take the medicine till then. That made Mandy feel a lot better. She says it's a deal. Maybe when I grow up I'll be the one to discover a cure—if they haven't already. Doc says we should try to understand how hard it is for Mandy when her controls get stuck. He asked Mandy if she could think of a way to make me feel better too. Mandy says maybe she can replace my car. Dr. Michaels is my kinda' guy! Mom invited Allison and her mother over tomorrow for lunch. Sweet!! I think it's time we go home Max.
Feeling Better,
Rick

Got a surprise this morning Max! There was a gift outside my door when I woke up. I knew it was from Mandy because the wrapping was lopsided and it had a lot of tape. I was hoping it was a new Turbo Max car but I should have known better. Mandy doesn't have enough money for that. She gave me her old remote control car. It's not very fast and it's pink with flower stickers on it! I can just see Ryan Harris laughing at my pink flower car while I finish last place in the next race. Mom says I better say thank you because Mandy's doing the best she can. I gotta get dressed now. I don't want Allison to see me in my pajamas again! I'm sure she'll be impressed with my new, slow, pink, flower car!!

New Car Owner,

Rick

I'm in a new club, Max. You're kinda in it too. So is Allison and Mandy. It's the Turbo Max Club. Everyone is helping me get the car in shape for the last race of the summer. Dad's going to help me boost the engine so it goes faster. Mandy's drawing a new design for the body and Allison's helping me paint it on. I think that will be my favorite part. We don't have much time so Allison will try to come over everyday to help. She said my red racer shirt is way cool!

Club Member,

Rick

My car will never be done at this rate, Max! Even with Mandy taking her medicine, it's really hard to work together. If things don't go her way we end up in a big fight. Allison hasn't been able to come over for the past two days. It's starting to look like the Turbo Max Club isn't a club after all. Mom says the support group meeting tonight is going to give us ideas on how to get along. Doc is coming to talk to the group. If we don't find a way to get along soon then my last hope for racing will be gone.

Desperate,

Rick

Doc was great as usual Max. I got a few ideas on how to get along with Mandy. You see, she gets frustrated really fast over little things. Doc says people with bipolar disorder have trouble when they are frustrated or stressed out. That's for sure. Mandy is just like that! Doc says when I see Mandy starting to get frustrated that I need to back off and help her handle the frustration. He says it's not the same as losing an argument. It's staying in control by deciding not to make a big deal out of something that's making her stress out. Sometimes it just means leaving her alone for a little while or taking a break and getting a drink or a snack. He says it's better to talk about things later when Mandy's not frustrated. I told Doc about the car project and our new club.

He says maybe Mandy and I could work on it together ... separately. Weird idea but it might just work. We could each do our parts at different times or in different rooms. I'm excited to try it out. Maybe my car will get done after all. Allison says she'll be over tomorrow.

New Ideas,
Rick

The Turbo Max Club is back in business, Max! One more good day like this and the car will be done. Sweet!! It was great having Allison over. I made a list of stuff that Allison and Mandy could help with on the car. I let them each pick a job. Mandy couldn't pick, as usual. When I told her to hurry up, she started getting upset and frustrated. That's when I tried the new trick. I said don't worry about it, let's get a drink and maybe it will come to you. You wouldn't believe it, Max. It worked like magic! As soon as the pressure was off, Mandy knew exactly what she wanted to help with. Mom was happy because we weren't fighting. I was happy because we got a lot done on the car! I learned my lesson. Spend less time telling Mandy she's wrong about stuff + spend more time helping her get past her frustration = everyone happy! Tomorrow the paint goes on my car. Dad says he'll be finished with the new motor by the race on Saturday. Race day here we come!

Frustration Reducer,
Rick

Well Max, it's done!! What a beauty ... and fast too! Huge piece of gold. Allison painted Mandy's new design on today. It's perfect. Now for the race tomorrow. Everyone's coming! The members of the Turbo Max Club plus Gram, Mom, Dad, and even the Doc are all coming. I can't leave you out either Max. I'm going to bring you along. That way I can tell you what happens right away. I've waited for this all summer. Will it really work out this time, Max?

Wondering,
Rick

It's warm up time, Max. We're at the Hobby Shop. Not too many people here yet. I'm really nervous. Mandy is much better than last time we were here! I've already seen Ryan Harris. He can't race again because it's against the rules but his little brother is racing with the new Turbo Max he won last time. I know it's a fast car so it'll be hard to beat. My car looks awesome though. Allison and Mandy are really proud of it too. Hope I don't let them down. Everyone's counting on me to win.

Holding My Breath,
Rick

Bad news, Max ...

I don't know how I'm going to fit the trophy in our car!! Can you believe I won? No, we all won! You should've seen Gram cheering me on. Mandy and Allison almost knocked me over! They were thrilled. Mom, Dad and the Doc looked so proud. Got my trophy already. I still have to pick out my new car, then it's off to celebrate over a pizza!

Winner,
Rick

P.S. I'm glad you were
here with me today, Max!

━━━━━ ▭ ▭ ━━━━━ ▭ ━━━━━

What an awesome day, Max. I can't even sleep just thinking about everything. The celebration party was a blast! The whole day was a big piece of gold. But something weird happened when I went to pick out my new Turbo Max car. All summer I dreamed about that moment. I was sure I knew exactly the one I wanted. But when I was standing there trying to pick, the whole summer ran through my brain—toothpaste everywhere, Gram's house, the hospital, not racing, bipolar stuff, meeting Allison, bad batteries, Mandy's medicine, smashed parts, the Turbo Max Club, frustration, and finally winning ... together. Then I knew which car to pick. I wouldn't let anyone see my choice. Have to wrap it first. I'll try not to get it lopsided or use too much tape. You can know my secret. The new car is pink with flowers. Mandy's going to love it! Now I know for sure Max—life is full of gold if you just know where to look for it!

Found My Gold,
Rick

P. S. School starts
Monday! (Yuck)

To My Lost Friend Max,

I can not believe mom found you! How did you get in a box up in the attic? You've been gone for so long. I looked everywhere trying to find you. I'm going back to school in a week but not to the 5th grade. I'm packing for college! There's so much to catch up on. Mandy graduated last year. She's had lots of ups and downs but she's learning how to manage her illness. She takes her medicine and makes her own doctor appointments. She's working part time as an apprentice at a local jewelry store. The owner loves her designs and she can work at her own speed. Allison and her family moved away two years ago. We keep in touch. She got really overwhelmed when she had to start at a new high school so she took her GED. Now she's taking writing courses at a local college. I just know she'll write a great novel some day. You should see her poetry. One time I asked her what it really felt like to be bipolar. She wrote an amazing poem! I'll show it to you. Mom and Dad run the support group now. Gram bakes the cookies for the kids. I come and talk to them about how to get along together. I tell them things I've learned like: "Don't push each other when you're frustrated" and "Look for the gold in each other." Dr. Michaels is still my favorite Doc. He takes great care of Mandy and always listens if I need help dealing with anything. He says I would make a great doctor. I talked to him recently about my decision to go to college. Mom and Dad wanted me to go but I was kind of afraid to leave Mandy alone. The truth is I was also a little afraid to go away myself. Doc says it's great that I want to help Mandy and there are many ways I can, but I shouldn't give up my life either. He said I should pursue the things I love. In some ways, that will keep me happy and healthy enough to be there for Mandy when she really needs me. That made sense to me. Now there's only one question left—what to do with the rest of my life. Well, I guess I'll figure it out as I go and by the end I'll have a full pot of gold. One thing I know for sure, Max. You'll always be one of the biggest pieces!
Your Best Friend Always,
Rick

Living Bipolar

The sweeter the gain
The greater the pain

The higher the thrill
The deeper the spill

The brighter the light
The darker the night

A total eclipse
Of the neuro-solar

That's what it's like
When you're living bipolar.

CPSIA information can be obtained
at www.ICGtesting.com
Printed in the USA
LVIC06n1215101015
457720LV00002B/2